P9-DWD-966

Princess Suque's Pony

Aleix Cabrera

Illustration: Rocio Bonilla

WINDMILL
BOOKS ™

Not all princesses
were born to sit still and follow the *Basic Manual of Royalty* word for word. Suque has always thought that these words were not made for her, and she daydreams.

The little princess often dreams of traveling beyond the Kingdom of Water. She wants to leave those small islands behind to face the dragons that are terrorizing villages and towns. She is convinced that she alone **will be able to tame and domesticate them.**

But to set out on this adventure,

beyond the world of fish and coral, she needs a pony. "When you are ten years old, you'll have one," the grown-ups always tell her. Times flies by, and now there is just one week left before her tenth birthday…

Then Princess Suque surprises everybody.
"What do you mean you don't want a pony?" exclaims the Queen, not understanding.

"You've always told us you want **to gallop off on adventures!" says the King.**

splish

splash

On the Isle of Fragua,
her uncle and seven freckled cousins

don't understand either.

"So, don't you want to save princesses from great danger anymore?" they ask her, one after the other, while her uncle hides the riding bridle and stirrups.

Her quadruplet aunts, who barely fit on their island, stop sewing the riding dress and cape. They are also taken aback.

"And who will tame the beasts then?"

Click!

Clack!

Click-clack!

On the next island,
her grandfather grumbles and stops
polishing the riding saddle that he was cleaning eagerly.
"I thought you would gallop all over the world, and
when you returned, you would tell me what it's like."

"Well, what do you want for your birthday then?" they all ask her. "A bridge. Well, lots of them," replies the princess without hesitating at all. "I would like them to join together **all the islands in the Kingdom of Water.**

The princess asks her grandfather for a suspension bridge, because the people on his island know how to work wood and leather. So the locals cut and tie together loads of planks and finish the bridge in the wink of an eye.

"Would I be able to work like that?" she asks herself.

Suque asks her quadruplet aunts, who barely fit on their island, for a crane with a basket large enough for her and another person to fit inside. And the aunts **surround themselves in ropes, string, and pulleys.**

20

Weee!

Tweet

Tweet

Tweet

Her uncle and seven freckled cousins are given the task of building the forged iron bridge. Their island of bare rocks is soon connected with that of the royal palace. From now on, they will no longer have to row from one island to the other!

The King and Queen have a very long stone bridge
built, to join the Kingdom of Water with the mainland.
"Why didn't we think of it before?"
they ask themselves.

25

"Now you can bring me the pony!"** exclaims the princess.
"Luckily we kept it in the palace stables!" says the King, very surprised.
"My girl, there's no way of understanding you!" sighs the Queen.

The princess hugs her new friend and then looks at her parents. "A horse, no matter how small, must trot very far. My pony must feel free and not imprisoned on an island.

That's why I wanted bridges and a crane with a basket!"

The King, the Queen, the

uncle, the seven freckled cousins, the quadruplet aunts, and the grandfather realize that Suque has given them all a present: the freedom to move from one island to the next.

"Let's go, my friend!" says the princess to the pony.

"A great adventure awaits us!"

Published in 2018 by **Windmill Books**, an Imprint of Rosen Publishing
29 East 21st Street, New York, NY 10010

Copyright © 2018 Windmill Books

Text: Aleix Cabrera | Illustration: Rocio Bonilla | Design and layout: Estudi Guasch, S.L.

CATALOGING-IN-PUBLICATION DATA

Names: Cabrera, Aleix.
Title: Princess Suque's pony / Aleix Cabrera.
Description: New York : Windmill Books, 2018. | Series: Little princesses.
Identifiers: LCCN ISBN 9781508194613 (pbk.) | ISBN 9781508194019 (library bound) | ISBN 9781508194651 (6 pack) |
ISBN 9781508193975 (ebook)
Subjects: LCSH: Ponies--Juvenile fiction. | Princesses--Juvenile fiction.
Classification: LCC PZ7.C334 Pri 2018 | DDC [E]--dc23

Manufactured in the United States of America
CPSIA Compliance Information: Batch BW18WM: For Further Information contact Rosen Publishing, New York, New York at 1-800-237-9932